Who Tops Who?

"Theresa" -- Richard admits to boorish behavior, but Theresa has no use for his apology. Then, he persuades her to accept a ride home from him and proves his integrity.

"FemDom Fairy Tale" -- A FemDom's offhand remark about a photograph at an erotic art show draws a handsome man's attention. But, when two dominants find each other attractive, which one chooses to kneel? (First published in Desire Presents.)

"Chocolate Cake" -- Her submissive toys wait for her at home, but Louise finds an offer by an attractive Dom as tempting as "Chocolate Cake." (First published in One Night Only: Explicit Erotica, edited by Violet Blue.)

"Switch" -- Liza found it difficult to maintain control around Emanuel, but she found his offer to share his slave with her irresistible.

I.G. Frederick trades words for cash, specializing in erotic fiction and poetry since 2001. Her erotic short stories appear in Hustler Fantasies, Forum, Foreplay, and Desire Presents, as well as electronic, audio, and print anthologies. Her novels receive high praise from readers, critics, and other authors.

A FemDom, Ms. Frederick, owns the man she adores. Although dominant in the rest of his life, he demonstrates his love by serving as her submissive. Ms. Frederick often writes about finding love in BDSM relationships from the authority of one enjoying that for almost a decade.

http://eroticawriter.net/

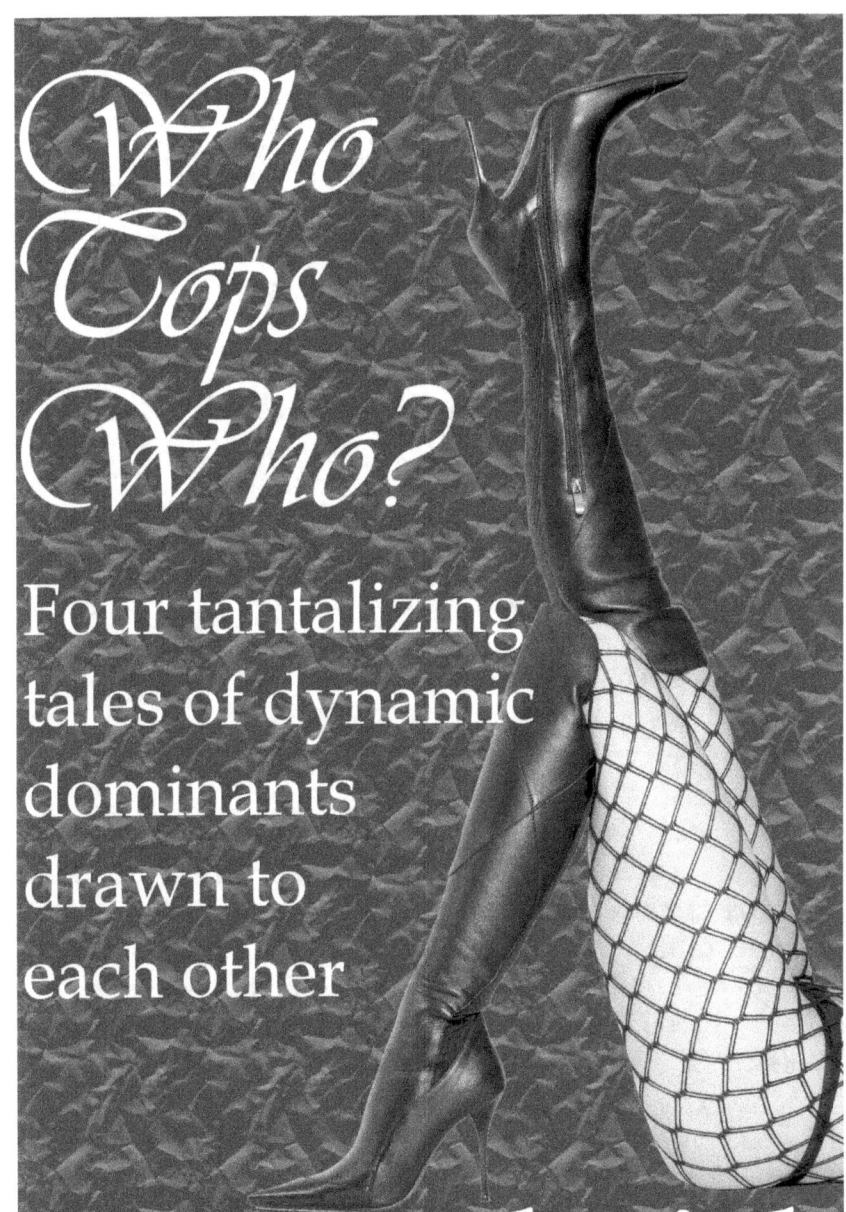

Who Tops Who?

Four tantalizing tales of dynamic dominants drawn to each other

I.G. Frederick

Author of Love Hurts & Dommemoir

Who Tops Who?
© **2014 by I.G. Frederick**

ISBN: 978-1-937471-34-7

Pussy Cat Press
http://pussycatpress.com/publisher.html/
P.O. Box 19764
Portland OR 97280

First published electronically in 2014

"Chocolate Cake" first published in *One Night Only: Explicit Erotica*, edited by Violet Blue , January 2012
"FemDom Fairy Tale" first published in Desire Presents BDSM 4.3

Table of Contents

Theresa

By I.G. Frederick

One pair of eyes caressed Theresa's skin, but she couldn't sort through the crowd to figure out who they belonged to. She concentrated on the whip in her hand and the naked boy bound in front of her on the cross, staying alert for those who strayed close enough to her scene that they risked a painful leather kiss.

She hated playing in public -- too many lookie lous; too many asshole Doms hitting on her, thinking because she was tiny they could make her kneel; and too many newbie idiots who didn't know enough to stay out of range of a six-foot signal whip.

Raising her whip above her head to avoid yet another careless voyeur, she added one more stripe to the dozens of welts across Jon's back and stepped closer, looping her whip across her palm. She released the winch to lower the cuffs holding his hands above his head and pressed against him, using her body weight to keep him from falling backwards. Removing the cuffs, she dropped them into the small duffle by his feet. He could clean them, and the whip, tomorrow.

"Can you walk?"

He pressed his lips together, then nodded.

Theresa slipped the whip into the bag, zipped it, and pulled the strap up over her shoulder. She put her right arm around Jon's waist and held his left hand in hers, guiding him to the chairs surrounding the snack table. When she had him settled onto a towel-covered seat, she retrieved a bottle of water and a paper cup full of trail mix and sat down next to him. While Jon munched and sipped, Theresa stroked his soft, greying hair.

A tall, muscular man with dark brown, almost black hair and a diamond in his left earlobe, plopped into the chair beside her and stretched out his long, leather clad legs. "I take it you're a service top?"

Theresa stared at him.

"It's obvious, you gave that boy everything he wanted."

She grimaced. "It's his birthday and he begged for the privilege of buying me a new dress and taking me to this party."

The man stared down the low-cut neckline of the figure-hugging red dress Jon had purchased. "And, what did he do to deserve such a delectable present?"

"Not that it's any of your business, but he cleans my house every week, does my nails, washes my hair." Theresa glared at him.

"Oh, you're a pro?"

"I take it you've never met a FemDom before." She spat out. "Let me guess, you're an online bottom and this party is your first real life experience." She turned in her seat so her back was to the interloper.

"My apologies." The deep voice penetrated the techno music that set the beat for the players in the dungeon.

She ignored him.

"I know, and am friends with, many FemDoms. I was just hoping, despite the evidence, that you weren't one."

He rose and stepped in front of her, squatting down between her and Jon. "I also do not wish to interfere with this man's aftercare. But perhaps you would consider allowing me to buy you dinner some night this coming week to make up for my boorish behavior."

She leaned away from him, as far back as the chair would allow, and stared, taken aback by his audacity and, she had to admit to herself, his rugged good looks. "If you do not leave me alone, I will ask the Dungeon Monitor to eject you from this event."

Every muscle in his face turned down and the sadness in his rich brown eyes almost made her reconsider. "My apologies." He stood and walked away.

Theresa expelled the breath in her lungs that she hadn't realized she was holding.

"I'm sorry, Mistress," Jon whispered.

She pulled him into her arms. "It's not your fault."

Theresa stepped into the back room and scanned the crowd of men and women, most wearing street clothes, a few in fetish garb. Seeing no sign of the boy who had courted her online and promised to meet her at the munch, she slipped into a corner booth, hoping to remain unnoticed. She saw none of her friends and no one she cared to get acquainted with. In the past few years, she'd become a recluse, avoiding community events, only playing with a few close friends at their homes or hers, accepting service from a married man whose wife couldn't understand his needs.

Numerous online conversations ended when she suggested a real life meeting, or worse they made a date and stood her up. She expected that outcome tonight and positioned herself where she could watch the door in hopes of seeing someone she knew who would enjoy sharing a drink with her.

But the only familiar face that entered the dimly lit, wood-panelled room was the prick from the party she took Jon to for his birthday. Theresa snatched up the menu and held it in front of her face, pretending to read the wine list.

"Mind if I join you?" He stood, blocking her ability to exit the booth.

"Yes, I do. Very much." She set the menu down on the table and tried to signal the harried waiter entering from the bar with a tray full of drinks. "I'm waiting to meet someone."

"Birthday boy?"

"It really is none of your business."

He bowed his head. "I know. And, I know you don't owe me the time of day. But I would really like an opportunity to make amends for the other night and let you see that I'm really not an asshole."

"I don't care one way or the other. I would just like you to stop bothering me."

"Look. I'll make a deal with you. Let me buy you a drink, right here at the munch where everyone can see us. If I can't convince you by the time you finish it that I'm not a jerk, I promise to never approach you again without specific invitation."

The waiter chose that moment to appear at the table. Before she could say anything, the man ordered a whiskey sour.

"Rum. Neat." She could down that quickly and be rid of the schmuck.

The waiter disappeared before she could specify label. She sighed, knowing she would get a cheap, well brand.

Unfortunately, she hadn't taken into account the time it would take the single waiter, trying to serve a few dozen kinksters, to return with the drink. The son of a bitch sat down opposite her and leaned across the varnished, faux petrified wood table.

"I will apologize one more time for my inexcusable behavior the other night. I was so mesmerized by your beauty that I wanted desperately for you to be a submissive, or at least a switch, so I could court you. I was incredibly obnoxious. I made some insulting assumptions based on witnessing a scene between two people I knew nothing about." He hung his head. "And, here I am adding insult to injury by insisting you hear me out." He took a deep breath and slid out of the booth.

"Thank you for accepting my drink." He put a ten and a five on the table. "Please tell the waiter to keep the change and I hope your date will enjoy the whiskey sour. Since I can't convince myself I haven't been a dickhead toward you, I know there's no hope of convincing you. I will keep my promise." He turned on his heel and trudged toward the exit.

Theresa stared after him eyes wide, mouth open. When the waiter set the drinks on the table, she handed him the money, put the shot glass to her lips, tilted her head back, and swallowed, letting the amber liquid burn its way down her throat. She shook her head. Well, at least she could hope the bastard learned his lesson and wouldn't afflict himself on any other unwilling women at future events.

After half an hour, she downed the whiskey sour as well and strode out of the restaurant into the cold rain. Alone as usual.

$\mathcal{C}$

A week later, Theresa couldn't believe she had agreed to come to the munch again in hopes of meeting yet another boy who sounded promising online. She swore to herself if this one didn't show up, she would close her account and just stop trying.

As she reached for the door to the back room, a long, muscular arm snaked in front of her hand and pulled it open. She looked up to see the handsome asshole holding the door ajar, standing as far away from her as it would allow. He nodded, but didn't speak. She shuddered and turned away from him, venturing into the room looking in vain for the man who had only sent her a photo the night before.

When she slid into the same booth, the waiter, balancing a loaded tray, dropped off a shot of amber liquid. "Rum, neat. From the gentleman."

Theresa sighed and took a sip, enjoying the rich smooth taste. At least he ordered the good stuff. Out of the corner of her eye, she saw the man talking to Angelo and almost dropped the glass. She hadn't seen Angelo in years, but had no desire to approach him while the degenerate was in the same proximity.

Fortunately, Angelo spotted her and, after exchanging a few words with the pilgarlic, approached her booth. "Theresa, darling. It's so good to see you out in the community again." Angelo kissed her fingers when she proffered her hand. "You look lovely as ever. How have you been?"

Theresa smiled."Not really participating in the community. Just here for a safe place to meet someone I corresponded with online and who's apparently stood me up."

Angelo slid into the booth across from her. "Still haven't found your pet?"

She shook her head. Angelo had been her mentor when she first entered the scene. "You set high standards. Haven't found anyone who lives up to them."

He laughed. "You actually met someone who lives up to them the other night. Just the wrong orientation. And, so smitten with your gorgeous self, he apparently made a complete jackass of himself. I offered to introduce Richard to you, who by the way I also mentored, but he believes he has eradicated any possibility of even becoming friends."

She nodded, but before she could speak, Angelo continued. "However, as a favor to me, I would appreciate you giving him a second chance, at least for a few hours. I'm only in town for the evening and I haven't seen either of you in a very long while."

Theresa looked around the room once more to prove that her date was a no show.

"He promises to be on his very best behavior."

She sighed and shrugged her shoulders.

Angelo turned to the dolt who leaned against the wall by the exit and nodded. The man strode over to the table as if he owned the joint. Theresa wished she could change her mind.

When he reached the table, he bowed from the waist. "Pleased to make your acquaintance, Lady Theresa. Thanks for allowing me to join you and our mutual mentor."

Angelo shifted further into the booth making room for Richard to sit on his side of the table. Theresa downed her drink and waved her empty glass at the waiter who brought her another and took orders from the two Doms sitting across from her. Even seated, they towered over her and she hated feeling vulnerable. She ignored Richard as much as possible, grateful that Angelo steered the conversation in neutral directions.

The room emptied over the hours and finally the waiter informed them that he needed to close up. Theresa pushed herself out of the booth and almost fell over. *Should NOT have ordered that fourth drink.* She looked up at the two men's concerned faces. "I'll be fine. Just stood up too quickly."

Angelo gave her what she always called his *No Way* look -- one eyebrow raised above the other, one fist on his hip. "You're drunk. How did you get here?"

"Walked over from the office. I can take a cab home."

Richard offered her his hand. "Please, Theresa. Let me drive you home. Least I can do."

Only the thought of trying to find a taxi in the rain when she could barely stand, made that thought appealing. She looked to Angelo who nodded. With a sigh, she took Richard's hand and had to force herself not to jerk it back. She stared up into his dark eyes and stifled a gasp. He just grinned.

Theresa let him steady her as they walked out of the restaurant. His touch made her melt. In the parking lot, she hugged Angelo goodbye and Richard handed her into his Acura. Except for giving him her address, Theresa didn't speak until Richard pulled up in front of her condo building. "I can manage from here."

He maneuvered into a parking space. "I'm not so sure about that. Please let me help you."

She took a deep breath. She had to admit, he was hot. And if they had sex, she could just chalk it up to being drunk. "I guess."

Richard helped her out of the car and kept his arm around her as they approached the building. He caught her keys when she dropped them trying to find the lock and helped her into the vestibule. He didn't try to kiss her on the elevator, probably because of the security cameras. When they reached her unit, he unlocked the door and guided her to the leather sofa in her living room. She was grateful to sit down so the room would stop spinning.

"Theresa, you are without a doubt the most beautiful woman I have ever met. I would very much like to have sex with you, but you're obviously intoxicated so all I can do is give you my number and beg you to call me when you're sober." He handed her a business card. The numbers were too blurry to read. He kissed the back of her hand, dropped her keys on the coffee table, and let himself out of the condo.

Theresa stared at the door, her mouth half open. She should have known. Anyone Angelo mentored would never take advantage of someone incapable of giving consent. She tilted sideways, brought her feet up onto the cushions and fell asleep, still clothed and wearing her boots.

In the morning, it took a shower and three cups of coffee before Theresa felt normal. She knew better than to have more than two drinks. Standing in front of the picture window that looked out over the river, trying to comb the tangles out of her waist-length hair, Theresa spotted the small white square sticking out from under the couch. She picked it up and turned it over. Obviously his scene card, it only had "Sir

Richard," an email address, and a cell number. She dropped it on the coffee table.

The card sat there for a week before Theresa decided to call. Of course, she got voice mail. "Hi. It's Theresa. Just wanted to thank you for the ride home the other night. And for being a gentleman." She hung up, feeling stupid, and tossed the card in the recycle bin.

Two days later, an unfamiliar number appeared on her cell while she let Jon worship her feet as a reward for cleaning her condo. "Hello?"

"Hi, Theresa, it's Richard. Sorry I didn't get back to you sooner, but I was down in the Bay Area this week. Would you consider going out to dinner with me?"

"Why?"

He chuckled. "Because I'm hoping you find me a little attractive and a bit intriguing and that you might consider having sex with me."

Well at least he was honest. "But, I'm a sadist."

"So am I."

"I've never submitted to anyone."

"Neither have I. But, we could have vanilla sex, no bondage, no pain, no power exchange."

She tilted her head. "Vanilla sex?" She watched the tips of Jon's ears redden. "I've never had vanilla sex."

"You're kidding?"

Theresa shook her head, even though Richard couldn't see her. "No. My first lover was kinky and he gave me a paddle as a present on our second date. In fact, he's the one who introduced me to Angelo."

Silence.

Jon looked up, his face red. "I should get home, Mistress. May I get dressed to leave?"

She nodded.

"Wow," Richard said. "I've never met anyone ... I mean, most people ... what ..." The phone went silent again. "I don't suppose you'd like to try it once?"

She shrugged. *I guess vanilla sex is better than none.* Aloud, she said, "I don't know. Maybe." He would call when she was all hot and bothered by foot worship from a man who could go home and fuck his vanilla wife.

"So, how about dinner?"

$\mathcal{C}$

Dinner was expensive and delicious and it could have been fish and chips at Burgerville. The only thing she saw was Richard's muscular chest under his black silk shirt. The only thing she smelled was the leather of his pants and the testosterone that rolled off him. The only thing she wanted to taste was his tongue in her mouth, even if she couldn't bite it.

He kissed her fingers during the appetizers, licked her neck during dinner, and nibbled on her ear through dessert. By the time the bill arrived, she was panting.

"Your place or mine?" He handed her into his Acura.

For some reason, the idea of sex without power exchange in her own bed was a real turn off. "Yours."

Richard owned a house in the west hills. After hanging their coats on a rack by the front door, he led Theresa up a carpeted staircase to a bedroom furnished in dark wood and leather. The covers pulled back on the king-sized bed revealed silky black sheets. Stepping up behind her, he wrapped his arms around her waist and dragged his tongue from the base of her neck to below her ear. "Should we get naked?"

She turned in his arms and looked up into his dark eyes. "No bondage? No pain? No power exchange? What exactly are we going to do?"

He laughed. "Well, see, I have this thing called a penis and you have this thing called a vagina and I would like to stick my penis in your vagina."

She gave him an exasperated *sheesh.* "I know that much."

"Wasn't sure. Don't know much about FemDom sex. Just don't expect me to ask for permission to come."

"At least warn me?"

"Sure." He tangled his fingers into her hair. She tilted her head back and he pressed his lips against hers. Her breathing, which had calmed to normal during the ride home, picked up its pace again. She parted her lips and his tongue explored the inside of her mouth. Her hands roamed across his broad chest and she found herself undoing the buttons of his shirt, eager to eliminate any barrier between her fingers and his skin.

His nipples were hard and she longed to bite them. She restrained herself and tweaked them with her thumbs instead. He inhaled sharply. She grinned. Causing a reaction was half the fun of hurting someone.

Richard's mouth moved from hers and his lips burned her neck. He reached back and slowly pulled down the zipper of her black sheath, revealing her naked torso, and gasped again. Pulling back far enough that he could slip her dress off her shoulders, he stared at her small firm breasts and the silky, dark curls between her legs. He ran one finger along the top of her thigh-highs. "Mind leaving those on for me?"

She shrugged and stepped out of the dress pooled at her feet. "As long as you're naked."

He chuckled and kicked off his shoes and pulled off his shirt, tossing it at the leather easy chair in the corner, then unbuckled his belt and unbuttoned his slacks. Slowly, he lowered the zipper. She stared, waiting. He let the pants drop to the floor with a clunk of wallet and keys. The tip of his hard cock peered out above the tops of his black bikini underpants and she sighed.

"What's wrong?"

"Just thinking how much I would enjoy torturing that."

"Sorry. Could say the same thing about your pretty, pert tits." He reached out and ran one finger from her chest to her nipple. She gasped.

He slipped off the briefs, grabbed a condom out of a night-stand drawer, and flopped on his back on the bed. "But, I'm sure you can think of other things to do with this." He rolled a red rubber over his prick. "Ones that don't hurt."

She grinned and planted her palms on either side of his legs, crawling up him until her pussy was just above his cock. "Torture doesn't have to involve pain."

"There's a difference between torment and teasing." He raised his hips so his glans nudged her lips, then dropped back. "And, two can play the latter game."

Theresa sank down on his dick and her eyes rolled back in her head. He fit perfectly, just thick enough to massage her g-spot. She rose up on her knees and slid down again. Richard reached up with one hand to tickle her nipple with his fingers. With his other thumb he massaged her clit. She clenched her cunt muscles. He moaned and pushed his hips up, plunging deeper into her. Bracing herself against his chest, her thumbs on his nipples, she pushed herself up and down. Richard increased pressure on her clit until the building tension shattered, her entire body shaking, her pussy clamping down on his dick.

"Consider this your warning," he growled. He grabbed her hips and furiously pumped up and down until he groaned and she could feel him pulsing inside her.

She collapsed onto his chest and he embraced her. When he slipped out, he rolled them both over so they lay on their sides, facing each other, chests pressed together, arms wrapped around each other.

When she finally caught her breath, she said: "Wow. I didn't know 'nilla sex could be that good."

"Chemistry, my dear. If you have it, any sex is fabulous. If you don't ..."

She had to agree with him. Despite Jon's devotion to serving her and his masochism, she had never wanted sex with him, even if he had been single. She limited him to foot worship as much because she could close her eyes and pretend someone else licked her toes as because that's where Jon's wife had drawn the line.

He put one hand on her cheek. "But, sex that good deserves more than a one-night stand, doncha you think?"

She wrinkled her nose. "Friends with benefits, maybe. But, I need someone in service to me, someone I *can* hurt.

He laughed again. She decided she liked the sound. "So do I. But, I never said anything about monogamy. Who knows, maybe we can find someone who will serve us both."

She shook her head. "Not likely. I'm straight."

He palmed one breast and pushed her on her back so he could lean down and drag his tongue across the other. "Fortunately, I'm not."

Theresa shuddered as much from the thought of Richard ramming into the ass of a boy licking her pussy as the sensation of his wet mouth caressing her nipple. She wrapped her leg around his muscular thigh and rubbed her clit against the hair-covered skin.

Chuckling, he grabbed her ass with his other hand, fondling her cheek. Her breathing, which had never quite slowed to normal, quickened again. "You'd like that, wouldn't you. Me fucking one of your pretty boys in the ass while he licked you? Sucking my jism out of your cunt after you and I fucked?"

He pressed his leg into her, but then pulled away from her. She whimpered, but it was only so he could grab another condom from the drawer. Once sheathed, Richard rolled on top of her and she opened her legs wide. With one hand on either side of her face, he leaned down and kissed her, shoving his tongue into her mouth at the same time he pushed his cock into her cunt.

Wrapping her legs around his waist, she slid her fingers through his long, dark hair, remembering not to stop and grab the strands. Her hands drifted across his powerful shoulders and she slipped under his arms to slide them around his back and pull him closer to her. So, this was the dreaded missionary position. She couldn't understand why folks derided it so. The muscles of his chest massaged her tits, his cock stroked the sensitive walls of her pussy, and his public bone rubbed her clit. Awash in sensual waves, her body floated in euphoria even as tension built. Her convulsions, muted by the weight of his body, reverberated through him and she found herself slipping from self identification into a duality she'd never experienced.

They exploded together, the intensity of her cunt's vibrations indistinguishable from the throbbing of his prick. She lost track of when orgasms morphed into aftershocks and her arms slipped from his back unable to maintain enough rigidity to keep them up. Richard kissed her lips, her nose, her forehead, then fell to his side, cradling her head on his shoulder, one arm flung across her chest. They were both panting. She tried to move her mouth, but she couldn't form words.

"Wow is right. I'm guessing you've never tried missionary before."

She managed to nod.

"More where that came from."

"Hmmmmm." She closed her horribly heavy eyes and was vaguely aware of Richard covering her with a sheet and blanket.

$$\mathcal{C} \; \mathcal{C} \; \mathcal{C}$$

FemDom Fairy Tale

By I.G. Frederick

In some ways, I'm every man's ideal slut. I'm always horny and I need almost no foreplay. Just stick a cock in my cunt and I come.

Only one problem: I'm a FemDom and a sadist. I want that cock attached to a man who will kneel before me in and out of the bedroom, who doesn't come unless I give him permission, and who can handle pain, lots of pain.

I look good in leather, but unfortunately, the only men I seem to attract are sissy boys who want me to make fun of their miniature meat. I want an *alpha* male who's proud of what he has in his pants and knows how to use it to please me.

I did my share of online. I can't even tell you how many twerps promised they would travel from all over the world for the honour of serving at my feet. With each successive dork, I became more and more skeptical and less and less open to electronic conversation. I got involved in the local S&M circuit. I volunteered, played at parties, put myself out there. All the macho men I met were either gay, already in service, or both.

Eventually, I resigned myself to spending my life alone and put my energy into my real estate career. I enjoy it, it's all-consuming, and, at least until recently, I made great money.

With the market in the toilet, I found myself with time on my hands. I spent a couple of weeks helping my best friend choose which three dozen of her hundreds of erotic photos to include in her solo exhibit at a swinger's club. I was thrilled that Andrea was finally getting the recognition she deserved, but was not so much about her invitation to attend the gala opening reception. I'm not a swinger and had never been inside a club. Still, after working with her, I wanted to see the display for myself and these days I never turn down free food.

When I asked her what to wear, she just laughed. "Leather, of course. There'll be all kinds of folk there, swingers, kinksters, etc. Just look hot."

I showed up in a leather over-the-bust corset that barely restrained my ample bosom and accentuated my narrow waist. A strip of leather that passed for a skirt flaunted my long, shapely legs. Garters peaking out below the skirt's hem held up black fishnet stockings. My knee-high, leather boots laced up the back. When I handed my black rain coat to the cloak room attendant, he whistled. I took a deep breath and ran my fingers through my long, straight, blond hair before stepping into the club.

Techno music reverberated off blood red walls. The room I entered had a long mahogany bar at one end and a dozen chest-high, circular tables scattered about, surrounded by polished chrome bar stools, most of which were occupied. A projector flashed Andrea's photographs above the door and I could see framed prints on various walls. Doorways led off into more rooms on either side of the bar.

I stopped and grabbed a glass of white wine, then wandered into the next room where guests helped themselves to crudités, puffed pastries, sushi rolls, and more treats covering several tables. Before I could grab a plate, Andrea's photograph of a gorgeous hunk of male flesh tied to a St. Andrew's cross grabbed my attention. She had captured the cracker of a four-foot snake whip caressing his erect cock. Even though I knew both the man on the cross and the whip thrower, who was not in the photograph, were gay, that picture always made me wet.

I sighed. "Why are all submissive males either sissies or gay?" I whispered under my breath.

"Most men are wimps when it comes to pain, anyway." I felt hot breath on my neck and turned to see a man who made the guy in the photograph look homely. "Are you the type of sadist who needs your bottom to enjoy pain, or can he just endure it?" He stood better than six feet tall, and his skin-tight leather pants and shirt revealed a powerful chest and strong arms. Dark blond hair brushed his leather-covered shoulders and even in the darkened hallway, I could see his eyes were sky blue. He had a six-foot signal whip coiled at his belt.

"Why do you ask?"

He dropped to one knee. "Because I smelled you become aroused when you looked at that photograph. And, although I prefer to be the one who doles out the pain, I have a very high tolerance." He looked me up and down so intensely, I could almost feel the heat of his touch. "I think I'd do almost anything for an opportunity to bed a woman such as yourself."

I raised one eyebrow. "I'm pretty deadly with a single-tail. And, I can throw it as hard as most men." Then it dawned on me. "However, I'm not a swinger. I'm only here because the artist is a friend of mine."

"I beg pardon if my words offended you, Miss." He rose to his feet and leaned over so I could hear him above the music's bass. "But, they were inspired by your appearance more than the surroundings." He held out his right hand. "I'm James. I would be very pleased to make your acquaintance and learn how you would prefer that I get to know you better."

"Christine."

His hand dwarfed mine. He turned his palm up and pressed his lips to my fingers. I had to reach for the wall behind me with my left hand to steady myself.

"You could come clean my house." I was kidding, but with my income halved by the economy, I could no longer afford a housekeeper. Since I had no one in service, I was forced to do my own housework and I hated it.

"Whenever you like, Miss."

I blinked and stared at him, but he appeared perfectly serious. "I require those who serve me to do so naked."

"That would make it even more pleasurable." He actually licked his lips and I shuddered at the thought of that tongue between my legs.

"You have experience?"

He shrugged. "I've lived alone and taken care of my own place for years. And, I presume you would train me in the way you wanted things done." His tongue emerged again and slowly drew a line from one corner of his mouth to the other.

Forget the housework, I thought. "Are you a member of this club?"

He nodded. "And, one of the rooms has a cross," he pointed to the photograph, "if you'd care to stay after the reception as my guest." He removed the whip from his belt, knelt, and held up his hands with the coils of the whip across them.

Torn, I hesitated. He lifted his hands a little higher. I reached out to caress the leather braids and somehow the whip ended up in my hand. I looked around, but didn't have enough room to throw it safely, so I just let the coils rest on my fingers. "I do need to find Andrea and I want to see the rest of the display."

"Rooms aren't available until after the reception and non-members leave. If I may," he replaced his whip on his belt. "I'll be most happy to carry this for you until then."

I nodded, at a loss for words, and moved to the next photograph.

Andrea found me there and gave me a hug. "I'm so very glad you could make it. Isn't it fab?"

"Very hot."

Andrea stared hard at James, and I knew she expected me to introduce him. But, I didn't want her to think we were in any way together. Someone else caught her attention and I moved on to the next photograph. James followed. When I took the last sip of my wine, he disappeared long enough to retrieve a refill. Then he presented me with a plate of hors d'oeuvres. "Since I'm not yet familiar with your preferences, I brought you one of everything."

While I munched first on a stuffed grape leaf and then a chocolate-covered strawberry, I encountered several acquaintances. Each time I could see questions in their eyes about the man who followed me about. I offered no explanation and they didn't give voice to their curiosity. When no one I knew was in hearing range, I sent him back for seconds on sushi, the crab in puffed pastry, and strawberries and told him to fill a plate for himself. While I nibbled from mine, he scarfed down what he had heaped on his.

"Hungry?"

"A bit. Didn't get lunch."

"Then, perhaps you should fortify yourself for what's to come." I pointed to the ladies room. "I'll be right back."

When I emerged, only Andrea and a few others remained and I realized the reception had ended ten minutes prior.

James stepped up to me and spoke loudly enough that the others could overhear. "Perhaps you'd like a tour of the club before you leave, Miss?" He winked.

"Sure." Andrea was engrossed in a conversation with the striking blonde who owned the club and I doubt if she noticed when we slipped through the door to the right of the bar.

The club wasn't as sleazy as I'd expected. The furniture was mostly pleather and chrome. Some rooms had windows opening to the hallway, others only doors, and one had a half wall all around with sofas and plush chairs positioned to accommodate voyeurs. The bed filling it could accommodate an orgy. A few of those who'd attended the reception lingered, lounging in the social area between the rooms.

James led me to a long room in the back with a picture window facing into the club. A St. Andrew's cross leaned against the wall at one end, suspension points were scattered across the ceiling, and a spanking bench sat opposite the cross. Three twin beds with tie downs at each corner lined the wall in between.

After closing and locking the door, James lowered the blinds across the window. With them half down he looked at me: "Unless you'd prefer an audience?"

I swallowed. "There are some things I don't do in public."

He laughed. "Thank you, Miss, for considering me worthy of that kind of attention."

He handed me the whip, and this time I uncoiled it and threw it in the direction of the cross. Impressed by its balance and accuracy, I snapped it so that it cracked.

James bowed. "Shall I strip?"

"Unless you want me to tear that leather off you, one lash at a time." I grinned.

He unlaced his shirt and raised it over his head, revealing tanned skin covered with only a small patch of hair between his nipples. I licked my lips. He hung the shirt on a hook on the back of the door and sat down on the floor to pull off his boots. When he pushed his pants down below his hips, he released an erection that made me want to throw him on one of the beds. After he hung up his pants, he kneeled in front of me and caressed the tops of my boots with his tongue.

Breathing heavily, I grabbed a fistful of his hair and pulled him up high enough for me to kiss him. He tasted of cinnamon breath mints and he welcomed my tongue into his mouth so I thrust it in deeper. Sucking on it, he slid his hands around to caress my ass. Unwilling to cede control, I pulled him to his feet and pushed him toward the cross. He obediently stepped up and put his arms into the restraints. I buckled the leather straps around his wrists and ankles and ran my hand along the firm globes of his butt before stepping back.

"How much warm up do you need?" I cracked the whip, just shy of his shoulders. He didn't flinch.

"If you start light, you can ramp up pretty quickly." He leaned his head forward between the arms of the cross.

I inched forward and swung the whip back and forth, stroking his beautiful ass without leaving a mark. Gradually I edged closer and increased the strength of my throws. His ass twitched, but I saw no other reaction. I put some muscle into my swing and a lovely red mark crossed his cheeks. He didn't move or cry out, so I threw again and again, pausing each time only long enough to make sure he didn't have a negative reaction.

I crisscrossed his ass and shoulders with pretty red marks while my thighs became wet and sticky. When I ran out of skin, I stepped up and drew my nails across the welts on his ass. His head fell back against my shoulder. I captured his mouth with my own and swallowed his moan.

Draping the whip between the arms of the cross, I unbuckled his ankles and then his wrists. I supported him with my shoulder under his arm and helped him walk over to the nearest bed. I expected him to flop down on his stomach or at least his side, but he eased himself onto his back and lay there with his pole pointing at the ceiling. I could no longer resist.

I snapped the velcro of the restraints around his wrists and grabbed a condom from the bowl on a small table next to the door. Panting, I sheathed him, threw one leg over his hips and sank my sopping wet cunt blissfully down on his thick cock. I exploded and fell forward, my breasts popping out of my corset and pressing into his chest.

Before I could recover, he picked up his knees and pushed upwards, again and again, sending my G-spot into paroxysms of pleasure. I clung to him while he slid in and out, making me come over and over and over again. I managed to lift my head high enough to reach his ear and grabbed his lobe with my teeth, clamping down hard. He didn't even slow down. I came again.

Putting one hand on either side of his head, I attached my mouth to his, letting him thrust his cock up into my cunt while I pressed my tongue down into his mouth. Neither of us cried out. The only sound in the room was our heavy breathing, and the slurping sound my cunt made as his luscious prick plunged in and out.

I think I'd come almost a hundred times when he turned his head a little. I released his mouth. "Please, Miss." His voice cracked. "I'd be most grateful if you'd consider allowing me to come."

I smiled. "Beg for it, boy."

I pushed myself upright. With my leather clad legs straddling his hips, I clenched and unclenched my pelvic muscles, watching his eyes open wide and a bead of sweat appear on his face.

"I'm begging you, Miss. I'm afraid I can't last much longer." He scrunched up his face. "If you won't let me come, at least stop doing that until I can regain control."

I laughed. "You'll come if and when I give you permission. I'm the only one in control here."

"Yes, Miss." A drop of blood appeared where he had bitten into his lip."I want to obey you, but what you're doing is driving me mad."

I dropped onto his chest and tilted my head back. "You may come, boy."

"Oh, thank you, Miss."

I sank my teeth into the strong muscles of his neck. He thrust upwards several more times, making me come one more time, and then exploded. His body went rigid and I could feel his cock spasm inside me.

Resting my head on his shoulder, I floated in post-orgasmic bliss, my pussy twitching. At some point, I realized he had wrapped his arms around me, although I didn't remember unfastening the restraints.

When his cock shrunk enough to slide out, he shifted so he could ease out from under me. I rolled over on my back, and he kissed his way down my neck, pausing to suck on each nipple in turn, then ran his tongue along the leather encasing me from the bust down. I opened my legs to allow him access to the sticky mess he had created. Dutifully, he licked my juices off my thighs then nudged my labia apart with his nose.

He lapped his way around my cunt and I trembled. When his tongue touched my clit, I exploded, and more juices gushed out. Gamely he fought a losing battle, trying to lick me clean while making me come again and again. Finally, when my clit couldn't bear any more stimulation, I grabbed his hair and pulled him up to lay beside me. He rested his head on my shoulder and put one arm under my breasts.

"I hope, Miss found my efforts pleasing."

I could only smile.

"And she'll tell me when she would like me to clean her house."

That startled me out of my euphoria and I turned to look into those beautiful baby blues. "You're serious?"

He shrugged. "I meant it when I said I would do anything to bed you. What I didn't realize was that I wouldn't be able to get enough." He stuck out his tongue and ran it the length of my upper arm. "I don't know that I'll ever get enough of this, and I realize that in order to keep me around, you probably want someone good for more than just whipping and sex."

I might have settled for that if money weren't so tight. But even if I could still afford a housekeeper, the thought of this man naked, on his knees, scrubbing my floors and toilet made me horny all over again. I ran my nails across his prick and gave him a wicked grin when it got hard again.

Chocolate Cake

By I.G. Frederick

Louise sat down on the worn sofa next to Maria and crossed one leg over the other. She set her mocha grande on the small rickety table at her elbow. Freedom of Espresso didn't have the most comfortable furnishings, but they made the best mochas in Renton. Louise always tried to indulge at least once on those rare occasions that she ventured back to the Seattle area.

"So, what have you been up to since I've seen you. Gracious, it's been years. Are you dating anyone?"

"Not exactly."

At that moment, Louise noticed a tall, blond man wearing an emerald green linen shirt that emphasized a muscular chest and powerful arms. He stood near the end of the coffee bar a few feet away. His eyes ran the length of Louise's legs from the strappy sandals up her firm calves to where her tanned thighs disappeared under her shorts. His gaze continued upward taking in narrow waist and the cleavage displayed by her half buttoned silk shirt.

She reached over with her left hand for her coffee cup. The man's eyes followed her movement and a smile played across his lips. He stepped to the side of the sofa, crouched down, and said in a soft voice impossible for anyone else to overhear among the coffee shop chatter: "I couldn't help notice the ring you wear." He looked at the gold triskeli on the middle finger of Louise's left hand and then up into her eyes. She found herself staring into the greenest pair she had ever seen. "May I assume you know the meaning of the emblem?"

Despite his quiet tone, his deep voice resonated through Louise. She nodded.

He reached out and traced the borders of the three interlocking patterns on the ring's face with one finger. "And that you wear it on your left hand deliberately?"

She nodded.

"Do you ever get involved with dominant males?"

Louise raised one eyebrow above the other.

He leaned closer and brought his lips near enough to her ear that she could feel his breath hot on her skin. "I am not submissive in any way, however I find strong, powerful women can be a real turn on for certain," he cleared his throat, "games. And I think you're very, *very* attractive." He let his gaze linger on her breasts and the two tiny keys that hung between them on the gold chain around her neck.

Louise turned her head so she could whisper in his ear. She inhaled the scent of male musk unembellished with any artificial odors. "I find strong, powerful men can be a real turn on for certain games and you're very attractive, as well. But, unfortunately I don't live here anymore, and I catch a flight early tomorrow morning for home."

The man smiled, revealing an even row of white teeth. "I don't want to interrupt your conversation any longer and I need to get back to the office for a quick meeting. But, I would love to buy you a farewell dinner this evening. If I give you my phone number, would you call me when you're done here? I work around the corner and could return within a few minutes."

Louise had planned to spend her final evening in town with her parents. She narrowed her almost black eyes a little. "If you give me your phone number, I'll call it later this evening. But, I'm afraid I won't have time for dinner. A drink after, perhaps."

He stood up, went to the counter, grabbed a napkin, scribbled on it, stepped back to the sofa and handed it to Louise. "This is my cell. I'd love to hear from you anytime before you leave town."

Louise looked at the phone number, folded the napkin, and tucked it into the breast pocket of her shirt.

"May I ask who will be calling me?"

"Lady Louise."

He reached down, took her hand in his, brought it to his face, and touched his lips to her ring. "Sir Peter so looks forward to hearing from Lady Louise."

He rose and grabbed a paper cup from the end of the coffee bar. The bells above the door tinkled as he left.

Maria stared at Louise. "Whatever were you two whispering about? Was that someone from your sordid past?"

Louise shook her head. "No, just wishful thinking on my part." She savored the complex chocolate and coffee mixture and wondered how Peter had picked up on her inconsistencies.

"So, I suppose there's no possibility of you hooking up with that guy later, falling in love and moving back up here?" Maria sipped from her clear plastic cup filled with ice and creamy Italian soda. "I've missed you."

Louise laughed. "He's hardly my type."

"Since when is a gorgeous hunk of manhood not your type?" Maria tilted her head to one side. "And what did you mean when you said you were 'not exactly' seeing anyone?"

Lowering her eyes to her cup to avoid Maria's gaze, Louise inhaled the fragrant steam. She and Maria had been best friends since high school. But she couldn't envision ever confiding that the preferred term for her current relationships was "in service" rather than "dating."

"Let's just say that I'm not looking for anyone at the moment." Even that, wasn't completely truthful. Although two men competed daily with each other for the honor of fulfilling her every whim, the keys she wore were to the padlocks that kept their cocks encased in plastic. And sometimes she wanted more than a male who would lick her for hours on end or take her strapon in his ass.

Louise knew it wouldn't be hard to sidetrack Maria if she encouraged her to talk about her own relationship. "Tell me about Jonathan." By the time Maria had shared every detail of her life with her new beau, their allotted two hours had slipped away.

Louise negotiated her rental car back toward Bellevue. While waiting in traffic, she kept thinking about how strong Peter looked. During dinner, she managed to forget about him long enough to hold up her end of the conversation with her parents and brother. But, as soon as the meal ended, she excused herself. "My flight leaves early, I need to pack and get some sleep. I'll probably be gone before any of you get up in the morning, so I'll say goodbye now."

Once in her room, Louise pulled out the napkin and her cell phone. She dialed *67 before the number Peter had given her to mask her own.

"Good evening, this is Peter." His deep voice resonated through her and she imagined his hot breath caressing her neck.

"Hi. It's Louise."

"My dear Lady, I'm so very glad to hear from you. I hope you can spare some time for me before you depart for destination unknown."

Louise looked at her watch. "My flight leaves Sea-Tac in twelve hours. I need about half an hour to pack and another half an hour or so to drive to somewhere near there."

Peter chuckled. "You do me great honor, dear Lady. May I be so bold as to book a room at the Hilton?"

"I'll meet you in the restaurant there in an hour." Louise ended the call. Most of her things were already in her suitcase -- the drawers in her parents' guest bedroom were full of their off-season clothing. She changed into her travel outfit: closed sturdy shoes, jeans instead of shorts, and a denim jacket over the silk shirt. *Not exactly sexy, but practical.* Retrieving her toiletries from the bathroom, she stuffed them into her oversized purse.

Her brother had already left for his home in Everett, and she could hear her parents settling in for the night. Louise unmade the bed so it would look slept in and snuck out the back door with her luggage. At the bottom of the hill, she hesitated. What was she thinking, sneaking out of her parents' house to drive to a hotel and meet a man with whom she had exchanged a couple of hundred words in a coffee shop? Yet, she headed toward the freeway entrance rather than return to the house. She pulled into the hotel parking lot with just enough time to make a pit stop before sashaying into Spencer's.

The moment she entered, Peter jumped up from where he lounged in one of the over-stuffed arm chairs across from the host stand. He kissed her hand and the touch of his lips on her fingers sent a charge of electricity racing through her, leaving every nerve tingling. Why had she decided to meet him in the restaurant rather than just go to a room? Oh, yes, negotiations. When he released her hand, she stuck both in her jacket pockets and stiffened her spine. They followed a waiter to a corner booth at the back of the dimly lit restaurant.

"Since you've already eaten dinner, how about dessert? They have a marvelous chocolate and fudge cake, perhaps with a glass of port?"

Louise smiled. "Chocolate cake yes, port no." She slid into the booth, deliberately staying near the edge, forcing Peter to sit opposite her, a large round candle flickering in between them..

When the waiter returned, he set a large piece of chocolate cake centered in a pool of hot fudge with a scoop of vanilla ice cream on one side and whipped cream on the other, in front of Louise. Peter slid around the table to sit next to her and picked up one of the two spoons from the plate. "I was hoping you'd share."

She nodded and dipped her own spoon into the cake, scooping it up with some of the fudge, ignoring the sweet white accompaniments.

"Besides," he dug into the ice cream, "I don't think you want our discussion shared with the wait staff." He winked.

Louise let the velvety chocolate melt on her tongue and savored its richness.

"Perhaps you'd like to specify exactly what types of games you enjoy playing with dominant males?" His hot breath against her skin sent waves of desire through her.

Louise grounded herself with another mouthful of chocolate delectability before responding. "I don't like pain. Bondage is okay, if it's not too tight. I won't accept any form of humiliation play, you can't tear my clothing, and I do not do anything submissive." She turned to stare at him while she stuck her tongue out to lick the chocolate off her spoon with the tip of her tongue in slow sensuous strokes. "But, you're bigger and stronger than I am, and I couldn't stop you from fucking my brains out, even if I tried."

Peter's smile made his eyes sparkle in the candlelight. "I see. Any physical limitations or medical conditions I should be aware of?"

She shook her head.

"Anal?"

She grimaced and shook her head more vigorously.

"Oral?"

Louise sunk her teeth into another spoonful of cake. "I bite anything that goes into my mouth."

"Gags?"

She shrugged. "Ambivalent."

"Hair pulling?"

"No pain."

He reached behind her and his fingers caressed the back of her neck. Then he bent them into her hair, and pulled her head back onto his shoulder. "This okay?"

Louise felt herself getting wet. She never understood the pleasure she took in this type of sex. She controlled every facet of her world, including the lives of the two men in her service. But sometimes, when the right man made himself available, she just liked to let go and let him take over. She smiled.

Peter leaned over and captured her lips with his own. His tongue took possession of her mouth and she pushed closer. He pulled away, frowning. "I thought you would fight me off."

She opened her eyes wider. "Not here."

"Safeword?"

She couldn't think of anything and wondered if she would be able to use one when he had already gotten her so aroused. "Chocolate cake."

Hot breath on her ear made it difficult to parse his next words. "Then let's go upstairs."

She nodded. Peter pushed her out of the booth, his hand still caught in her hair. He tossed a folded-up bill on the table, grabbed her purse, and guided her through the nearly empty restaurant toward the elevators. When the doors slid shut, he pressed her against the wall with his body and kissed her again, hard. His hand slid inside the waistband of her jeans and his fingers found their way between her legs. He chuckled deep in his throat when he discovered how wet she'd become, his laughter rumbling in his chest.

He strode down the hallway of the fifth floor pushing Louise in front of him. She struggled to keep pace, worried someone might misinterpret their body language. Before she could even see the room number, he had a door open and thrust her inside. He paused long enough to turn the safety latch and toss her purse onto the desk chair. Then, he threw her onto the softness of the bed. She tried to get up, but he flipped her over on her stomach and used his belt to bind her wrists behind her back. She twisted away, but that only made it easier for him to remove her shoes and unbutton her jeans.

"No," she shouted. "Stop."

"Hell no." Peter's voice had deepened and sounded ominous, sending a thrill of fear down her spine. "You're mine until your flight leaves, assuming I'm done with you by then." He pulled her jeans and panties off together.

She tried to crab walk away from him, but he grabbed her ankles and yanked her legs apart. Using his pelvis to hold her in place, he unbuttoned her shirt and undid the front hook on her bra. Still clothed, he used his weight to keep her from escaping while he sucked on one nipple and forced his hand in between her legs. He rubbed her slick clit with his thumb until she stiffened, close to the brink. He stopped and she screamed in frustration.

"What makes you think I have any intention of letting you enjoy this?"

She opened her mouth to answer and he stuffed her panties, fragrant with her own musk, between her teeth, cutting off her response. Before she could spit them out, he tied them in place with a bandana. Still on top of her, he grabbed both her breasts, pinching her nipples between his thumb and middle finger. She squirmed, but he stopped just before pleasure turned to pain.

Damn, he's good, she thought in a moment of lucidity. "Stop it you bastard," she mumbled around the gag, making sure she could still safeword if she needed to. She very much doubted that would be necessary.

Without getting off of her, Peter managed to remove his pants and she heard the reassuring rip of a condom package, one thing she'd forgotten to mention downstairs. He shoved himself into her so hard, her head pushed into the down pillows leaning up against the wooden headboard. Her breasts jiggled up and down with his thrusts and once again, she found herself near the edge. She attempted to disguise her approaching orgasm by trying to squirm away, but he pulled out, leaving them both panting.

"Absolutely, no way." He flipped her over on her belly and piled the pillows under her stomach. "Not gonna happen."

Louise cried out, desperate for relief. Every inch of her skin burned with heat, her swollen clit ached, and her juices had soaked the bedcover and made her thighs sticky. Peter slammed into her again. She went limp, letting him fuck her, letting the tension build, she hoped, unnoticed. It took longer in this position, but his cock massaged her G-spot pushing her toward the edge again. When he pulled out this time, she sobbed.

"You're one hot little number aren't you?" He ran his palm across her ass cheeks. "Maybe I need to throw you in the shower to cool you down."

Louise knew no amount of cold water would ease the heat between her legs. She tried to rub her clit against the bed, but the pillows positioned her so she couldn't get any contact.

"No, you don't." He flipped her back over.

Pissed, she kicked at him, but he caught her leg with one hand. He produced a leather cuff with the other and buckled it on, then grabbed her other ankle. She discovered the cuffs were attached to chains. Her legs were now pointing at either corner of the bed and she had very little range of motion. Straddling her waist, his still-erect cock on her stomach, he reached behind her and removed the belt. He took off the rest of her clothing and produced two more cuffs. She tried to prevent him from capturing her wrists, twisting her upper body, pulling her arms out of his grasp twice. But her strength was no match for his, especially with her legs already bound.

He ran his hands up the length of her legs, across her hips, and up to her breasts. She squirmed. She needed to come so badly, she'd do almost anything to get relief. Except beg. He pulled his own shirt over his head without bothering to unbutton it and lay down on top of her. She pushed her hips up into him, but he kept his cock on her stomach, out of reach.

Laughing, he kissed her neck, her breasts, and nibbled on her ears. He dry humped her belly and for a moment, she feared he would come that way. Finally, when she worried that she would pass out from frustration, he slid back into her. He rammed himself in and out of her so hard, the bed shook and the headboard banged against the wall. The tension that had been building in her clit all evening became the only thing that registered in her consciousness. The heat of his skin against hers, his heavy breathing, the pressure from his cock thrusting into her, all just pushed at that tension. She couldn't hide what was happening anymore than she could shove him away and get off the bed. Her whole body stiffened, her pussy twitched and pulsed, and she exploded, sobbing with relief and ecstasy. She was vaguely aware of him shuddering inside her and the pounding of his heart against her chest. When her breathing had slowed to normal, he kissed her. She didn't remember him removing the gag, but she kissed him back. She had never had such an intense orgasm in her entire life.

Somehow, the cuffs were removed and she ended up under the down comforter, snuggled in his arms her head on his shoulder, her pussy still twitching.

"My flight..." panic surged through her for a moment.

He stroked her hair. "Don't worry pet, I set the alarm. You can get a couple of hours sleep."

She snuggled closer and closed her eyes.

Switch

By I.G. Frederick

Even in a crowded dungeon, I could sense his approach. I steeled myself to turn and face the onslaught from eyes the color of jadeite, reflecting his kelly green satin shirt. I tried to smile, but I think it emerged as a grimace.

"What's wrong Liza?" Emanuel stood with a magnificent black Morgan bullwhip coiled across his palm, his other hand pushed against his leather-clad hip.

"What makes you think something's wrong?" I had to look up to see his face. I preferred tall men who knelt so I could look down at them.

He tilted his head and his silky, dark brown hair fell over one eye. I wanted to run my fingers through it until I got to the back of his neck then pull him down to his knees so I could talk to him properly. But, as the whip in his hand reminded me, he was as dominant as I, and he owned a gorgeous, petite blonde.

I cleared my throat. "Something I can do for you?"

"Actually yes. I was wondering if I could persuade you

41

to go out for a drink after this. Unless you're going to the party?"

I shook my head. None of my regular toys were available and I hadn't felt like paying twenty bucks to go stag. "You aren't taking Felicia?"

He sighed. "She's filling in at the crisis center tonight and won't get off until seven in the morning."

"I suppose you won't give me a hint?" Emanuel was one of the few dominant males I knew who had never hit on me, so I figured I was safe from him. Myself? Well that was another matter entirely.

He glanced around the room full of kinksters perusing tables laden with whips of every configuration; piles of rope in myriad colors; leather fashioned into cuffs, corsets, binders, blindfolds, harnesses, clothing; wood shaped into paddles, stocks, humblers; and metal insertables, cock rings, pinwheels, claws, chastity devices, collars. Along the wall, cages, crosses, and suspension rigs tempted buyers. Apparently he'd had enough spare green to acquire a thousand-dollar whip. Even though I had a decent job now, getting laid off three times in two years made me leery of expensive equipment when I only got to use it at the occasional party.

"Indulge me?"

It's not you I'm worried about. I sighed. "I guess." It was Saturday afternoon and I had nowhere else to go for the evening.

He barely smiled, but his eyes sparkled with anticipation. *What have I gotten myself into?*

"Most of the places in this neighborhood are dumps. Do you mind driving somewhere?"

I shook my head. *Who drives to the convention center?* "I took the Max."

This time he grinned. "So did I. We could take it downtown."

"Sure. I'm done here."

He lifted the whip high enough that I could smell the

kangaroo leather. "So am I. Put everything I brought to spend into this. Besides, I have most everything I would want that's available for sale here." I could have sworn he stared at my tits. Granted, I flaunted them with a pushup bra under a black silk shirt opened to the third button. Although I couldn't be sure he wasn't just admiring his purchase, his gaze made me want to come up with an excuse to get out of this encounter.

We stopped at the cloak room and Emanuel grabbed my leather coat from the volunteer before I could take it and held it out for me to put it on before accepting his own black leather jacket. I was impressed that he managed to get it on without putting the whip down.

Is the man going to walk onto public transit carrying a ten-foot bullwhip? Is that even legal?

The volunteer handed him a black leather messenger bag. He held a folded five dollar bill over her impressive rack that made mine look puny. She wiggled permission and he tucked it in between her breasts before putting the bullwhip into his bag.

Okay, the guy just likes big titties. I can live with that. Felicia's small breasted, so apparently Emanuel doesn't pick his women on looks alone.

Since the Green line showed up first, we settled on walking back to Bailey's Taproom on Broadway from the stop at Fifth and Oak. The place was starting to fill up, but we scored a table along the wall of windows overlooking Ankeny Street. I slid onto the bench seat facing the bar and scanned the screen listing beers available from the impressive row of spouts behind the bartender.

As I settled on a Hilliard's *Murdered Out Stout* that had just been tapped, Emanuel, who was still standing, asked, "Can I buy you a beer?"

He returned with two tall glasses, his beer dark but mine darker, and slid in next to me ignoring the chairs on the other side of the table. I sniffed at my glass and the aromas of vanilla and caramel mingled with the leather scent emerging from our clothing. I sipped, tasting hints of chocolate and coffee in a porter brew. *Should have specified the small pour.*

Emanuel took a long swallow, licked his lip and turned to me. "I've accepted a new position that starts next month. I'll be traveling a lot more than I do now and I don't want to leave Felicia alone for weeks at a time."

Every muscle in my body tensed and I prepared to bolt for the door.

"I want to find another girl, but Felicia's my alpha so it would work best if she could top the new girl."

I raised one eyebrow higher than the other, a look that put most of my toys on their knees if they weren't there already. Emanuel didn't even flinch.

He leaned closer and whispered in my ear. "I was wondering if you would be willing to mentor Felicia and teach her how to dominate another woman."

One by one my muscles relaxed and I guffawed. I rested my forehead on my hand, but I couldn't stop laughing. My entire body shook, my tits almost popping out of my bra. I finally gained a semblance of control and wiped one finger under each eye to control the tears.

I leaned close enough to inhale a whiff of his skin and the pheromones raced straight to my clit. I tried to ignore them. "You've got to be kidding? Felicia's adorable, but she couldn't top an eager dog."

He hung his head. A moment later he took another long swig of his drink. "Do you find her attractive?"

Actually, I had the hots for her as much as I did for her Master. I nodded and took another tiny sip of my beer. I definitely needed to stay one hundred percent sober for this conversation.

He stared into his glass for a moment, then turned those mesmerizing eyes my way. "Felicia has confessed that she thinks you're, in her words, "hunky." I've watched you play and I've seen how you treat your toys. If we could negotiate terms satisfactory to us both, would you consider some kind sharing arrangement?"

I was grateful my glass sat on the table. I suspect if it was in my hand at the moment I would have dropped it. As it was, I just stared at him.

He leaned over. "The reality is the only other woman I might be interested in is unavailable for ownership. Felicia needs to serve almost as much as she needs pain. And, she's had to severely curtail her public activities because of her job."

I had noticed I'd seen less of her this past year. I'd even wondered if the two of them split up, except he always mentioned her in conversation and I'd seen them together in vanilla settings.

"If I'm going to be gone half the month, she will need someone else in her life. I could never share her with another man. But, another woman ..."

I let out a breath I hadn't realized I was holding and took a long swallow while the pros and cons raced through my head. I had been single for almost three years, resigned to only playing at parties and limited sexually to electronic pleasure devices. If Emanuel's main goal was to provide Felicia with someone to serve while he was gone, my interaction with him probably would be fairly limited. That would save me from the risk of doing something one of us would regret. Somehow if I came up with any cons, I forgot them immediately.

"It's an interesting proposition. I would be willing to discuss it further. But, I would like Felicia to be present for the negotiations so that she can express her opinion." Emanuel might have the right to give Felicia to me, but I only wanted her if she liked the idea.

"Absolutely." Emanuel extracted a phone from his breast pocket. "Why don't we have you over for dinner?" He scrolled for a moment. "How does next Friday evening look?"

I pulled my phone out of the hip pocket of my leather

pants and made a show of checking my calendar even though I had nothing scheduled. "What time?"

Emanuel owned a duplex in Northwest only a block from the street car. When I arrived, I climbed up the stone steps to the right door and rang the bell. It opened and I entered to find Felicia wearing only a garter belt, stockings, three-inch heels, and an apron that barely covered her flat tummy. Her long blonde hair was pulled back in a pony tail. I noted the blond curls between her legs both as verification that her hair was not dyed and in appreciation of the fact that Emmanuel didn't subscribe to the silly custom of making slaves shave. I liked my pussy in its natural state and if you shaved off all the hair, you couldn't pull it.

In addition to the steel ring around her slender neck she had, as I discovered when she turned to hang my coat on a tree next the door, a cursive E branded on her right hip.

The idea of owning someone who would accept my brand made me wet. So many wanted to limit that type of marking.

Felicia led me past an entrance on the left to the staircase leading to the upper unit — apparently Emanuel used both — through a hallway with doors on either side to a large open room. I had to resist caressing her tempting ass.

From the kitchen along one wall emanated tantalizing smells of garlic, butter, Parmesan, and chicken. A large, round cherry wood table stood between the kitchen and a sitting area furnished in overstuffed leather furniture facing a marble fireplace. Two wooden chairs with padded leather seats and armrests faced each other across the table and a third, smaller, armless chair with a towel across the seat had been placed between them.

Emanuel rose from an armchair so large I hadn't realized he was sitting there and set a tablet on a Queen Anne table next to it. He wore a white shirt with a high, open collar, and black dockers. When he strode toward me, I extended my hand to shake his. Instead, he turned it and pressed my fingers to his lips. I grabbed the back of the nearest chair to maintain my balance.

"Thank you so much for coming, Liza. I've let Felicia know why you're here and she's spent all day cleaning and cooking in your honor."

I smiled at the girl who did a curtsy so low her knees almost touched the floor. *Goddess she must be fun to tie up.*

"Thank you so much for taking Master's proposal under consideration, Lady Liza. Serving you would be such an honor." She rose to her full height, a good several inches taller than mine. Her pert breasts bounced gently with her movements and I licked my lips at the thought of torturing her lovely cinnamon-colored nipples. "If you'll excuse me Ma'am, dinner needs a bit more attention." She bowed and backed away until she reached the counter then turned and busied herself at the stove.

"Would you like a glass of wine?" Emanuel held out one of the two arm chairs.

I sat down, careful to avoid brushing against him. I was already wondering if I should have brought a spare pair of panties.

Unfortunately, after he pushed in my chair, he leaned over, his lips less than an inch from the skin of my neck. "You smell divine. I take it you appreciate our girl's attire?"

That's half of it. Aloud, I said, "She *is* lovely. And, yes, I would like a glass of wine."

By the time Emanuel had settled into the seat opposite me, Felicia emerged from the kitchen with a silver tray. She set one glass of white wine in front of me and put another in front of Emanuel, then placed an antipasto platter on one edge of the lazy susan built into the center of the table.

Emanuel turned the lazy susan so the platter was within my reach and raised his glass. "Please, help yourself."

I nodded and used the silver serving fork to take several

olives, a small pickled pepper, some prosciutto and a slice of provolone. I took a sip of the wine, a delightfully bright Riesling.

Emanuel turned the lazy susan until the platter was in front of his plate. "Why don't we start with your preferences for how this relationship might work?"

I nibbled on an olive, the salty tang sliding across my tongue. "A lot would depend on your limitations. I have a very small condo in the Pearl and no play equipment to speak of."

"After dinner I'll take you downstairs and show you my dungeon. You would be welcome to use it as much as you like. I only ask that Felicia or I be here if you bring other toys over, especially if they're male."

I wrapped the provolone around the prosciutto and bit off one end. "I only play with toys who don't belong to me in public. Especially males." At five feet barely, even though I had some martial arts training I could easily be overpowered by any of the tall, muscular men I preferred. Men like Emanuel. "I probably would only use the dungeon when you were out of town, anyway."

"I wouldn't want to limit you." He smiled over his wine glass.

Without color reflecting from his shirt, his eyes were almost grey but still enthralling. I had to grip the chair arm with my free hand. Once I got myself under control, for the moment, I pulled the ivory linen napkin from its engraved silver ring, used it to blot the salt from my lips, and spread it across my lap. "I would expect Felicia to obey me unconditionally in your absence. You and I will come to agreements about her limits and I will respect them. But, I would not be able to accept an environment where she would have any expectations of you countermanding an order I gave."

"If I may speak, Ma'am." Felicia stirred a large sauce pan on the stove in the island between the kitchen and the dining area.

Emanuel and I both nodded.

"If Master gave me to anyone I would expect to serve that person as if they owned me. I know he would never hand me over to anyone who might do me harm." She added something green to the pot and blushed. "Besides, I suggested that Master speak with you. I know he first talked of you mentoring me, and I'm glad that you convinced him how bad an idea that is."

She gave the pot another stir and turned to the oven built into the wall of cabinets. She extracted a large platter covered with pasta, set it on the tile countertop, and ladled sauce from the pot over it. "I suspect I will very much enjoy serving you, Ma'am." She batted her eyelashes. "Especially if you allow me to serve you in all ways." The blush now extended down her neck and across her delectable breasts.

I wondered if she might be on the menu for dessert. "Something tells me we won't need to spend much time on negotiations. Perhaps you should just review what your limitations on her use will be."

Felicia turned off the oven and pulled out a large bowl. She brought it to the table, set it on the lazy susan, and returned for the platter. A bouquet of garlic, olive oil, and onion emanated from one dish and garlic, cheese, and butter from the other.

I filled my plate with Alfredo covered ravioli from the platter and green beans stir fried with onions, garlic, and red peppers from the bowl. Felicia stood behind the third chair waiting for Emanuel's nod. She took her seat and sat with her hands in her lap until he turned the wheel so the pasta dish was within her reach. After he allowed her to put some green beans on her plate, she again sat with her hands in her lap.

After Emanuel and I had both eaten a bite, he said, "You may eat as well, girl."

"Thank you, Master, Ma'am."

I smiled at the inclusion then lost myself in rich pillows of pasta filled with creamy chicken and spinach and covered in sensual, cheesy sauce. "This is delicious. You made the pasta yourself, didn't you?"

Felicia smiled and bowed her head.

Emanuel raised his glass. "She's quite the cook." He took a sip. "If she doesn't know how to prepare something you like, she'll learn."

I bit into a crisp green bean, perfectly infused with the flavors of garlic and onion. *I could get used to living like this two weeks of the month.*

"Her limits are just the basics: no kids, animals, or scat." Emanuel's voice startled me out of my foodgasm. "Because of her job, any marks must be where she can hide them under clothing during the day. And, I would not permit any permanent marks although eventually, we could perhaps add something to her collar." He emptied his wine glass and Felicia jumped up and filled it.

I took advantage of the pause to indulge in another perfect piece of pasta.

"I would expect you to care for her as if she were your own property. I've watched how you treat even your playthings and whenever your name is mentioned, it is with respect and deference."

Which is why I'm still single. I nodded and lifted my glass. "I'm looking forward to getting to know Felicia much, much better."

They both raised their glasses as well, but I kept my eyes on Felicia to avoid her Master's mesmerizing gaze. I thought about all the painful things I could do to her beautiful breasts, the torments I could deliver to the luscious lobes of her ass, the agony I could produce between her legs. *I definitely should have brought a change of underwear.*

I indulged in more of the pasta than I should have if I had hopes of playing that evening. I was grateful when Felicia cleared the plates and no one mentioned dessert.

Emmanuel rose and offered me a hand. "Come, let me show you around the dungeon while Felicia tidies up and, if you have time, perhaps you could even indulge yourself. I know she would like that a lot."

She swayed her hips provocatively while she transferred our dishes from the table to the kitchen counter. But I was too distracted by my reaction to Emanuel's touch to really appreciate her offer. I let him pull me to my feet then withdrew my hand and stuffed them both in the back pockets of my black jeans.

He led the way back through the hallway to one of the closed doors. Opening it revealed a carpeted stairway, lit by faux candle, wrought iron wall sconces. At the bottom of the stairs, he hit a switch and lit up a cavernous room. The lighting was subtle. Recessed in the ceiling it illuminated the room without glaring.

Furnishings — including a Saint Andrew's cross, a bondage rack, a steel cage big enough for two to crouch in, full stocks, a Saint Catherine's wheel, a spanking bench, a bondage chair, a padded table, a leather love seat, and several chests of drawers lined three walls. The fourth displayed an impressive array of whips, chains, paddles, rope, cuffs, gags, blindfolds, binders, and chastity devices for both men and women hanging from hooks. The man could open a store.

Thick, well-padded black carpet covered the floor. The center areas were clear except for the support posts which had been padded and studded with tie points. The ceiling support beams had additional tie points, enough to suspend several people at the same time with room to swing a signal whip (but not the ten-foot beauty he had purchased at the vendor fair). Usually someone this well equipped hosted parties occasionally, but I'd never heard of one.

My eyes strayed back to the chastity devices. "You play with boys?"

He followed my gaze and bowed his head, his hair falling to obscure his face. "Please, Miss Liza, won't you sit down?" He pointed to the love seat and I sank into the comfy cushions. "First, I must ask that whatever occurs in this dungeon always be kept in strictest confidence, including any conversations. Any toy you bring here must also agree to that condition."

I nodded. His entire demeanor had shifted. I couldn't put my finger on it, I didn't know him well enough, but it was almost as if once we entered the dungeon together, Emanuel had left and some other man had taken his place.

"I owe you an apology."

Already? But no one's done anything yet. I just stared at him.

"I'm afraid I wasn't entirely truthful when I spoke to you the other night."

I was getting a crick in my neck looking up at him. Ever so slowly he sank to his knees in the thick carpet where his eyes would have been at my level, if he looked up. "I originally was hoping you would teach Felicia to top. But, not because I'm looking for another girl. I had wanted her to top me. I'm a switch, but I really don't want anyone to know that."

I may as well toss these panties in the dumpster on the way out. I swear I gushed as much as if I'd come. Visions of Emanuel flashed through my mind: naked, bound to the cross, my whip marking his back ... suspended from the ceiling while he swung back and forth from the force of my paddle against his ass ... tied to the table his balls bristling with clothespins, his cock bouncing as I struck it with a miniature flogger. I licked my lips.

"Reality is, I've wanted to play with you since the first time I saw you flogging a boy bound to a cross in the dungeon at WhipFest two years ago. But, I never had the courage to approach you and confess my attraction and my orientation."

I was grateful to be sitting down. Emanuel was one of the few men I believed incapable of submitting to a woman.

"If you're amenable, and if you're willing to keep my secret, I offer you a package deal."

I can't brag to my FemDom friends that I have the handsomest, domliest man in the local scene bottoming to me? Oh, wait, I don't have any FemDom friends. "Exactly how much of a package are we talking about? Are the two of you available for potential ownership?"

His head shot up and those fascinating eyes, now a pale blue, stared up at me. There was definitely someone else at home.

I crossed one leg over the other. "You're not just a switch, are you?"

Slowly he turned his head from one side to the other.

"How many?"

"Mostly it's just the two of us. I prefer to be called Eric, if that's acceptable, Ma'am."

"And, Felicia?"

"Oh, no, Ma'am. There's just one of her."

I laughed. "I meant, she knows about this, all of this?"

Emanuel/Eric nodded. "She's always known. She's a counselor and several of her patients have DID. She recognized it right away."

"And your counselor?"

"I don't have a counselor, Ma'am. Emanuel keeps things under control. I'm only allowed to come out to play. He rarely allows the others to do more than watch. The only problem, I'm afraid, is that I become more and more insistent the longer I don't get to bottom. I used to have a couple of discreet play partners willing to keep my secret in exchange for use of Emanuel's dungeon. I'm afraid that ended when Emanuel spotted you at WhipFest."

Emanuel spotted you. The implications of that wording were staggering. "And, what happens if Emanuel shows up when I'm playing with Eric?"

"Not likely to happen as long as I'm in some type of confinement."

"What about sex?"

"Ma'am, I offer myself to you under the same terms that Emanuel offered you Felicia."

I couldn't stand it anymore. I pushed myself to my feet, stepped in front of Eric, and grabbed his hair. Kneeling, he was almost as tall as me. I leaned down and pressed my lips to his. He opened them and invited me to ravish his mouth.

I sucked his tongue into my mouth and bit it. He moaned and leaned into me. I couldn't believe I had the body I had drooled over the past two years on his knees offering himself to me. At that moment, the icing on my cake arrived and knelt just out of reach. She sat with her ass resting on her heels, her hands palms up on her thighs, her head bowed. No longer bound, her blonde hair cascaded over her shoulders.

I pulled Eric's hair, tilting his head back so he had to look up at me. As gorgeous as Emanuel's hazel eyes were, I much preferred looking into Eric's blue ones. The adoration and eagerness made me tingly all over. "You have clothes on, boy. When I'm in this dungeon, I expect everyone else to be naked. Always." Hopefully, that alone would discourage Emanuel from showing up.

"Yes, Ma'am." He unbuttoned his shirt. "May I stand to undress?"

I released his hair, stepped over to Felicia, and grabbed hers. "Yes." I leaned down and kissed her sweet lips. She tasted of peppermint, she must have stopped to brush her teeth before joining us. I became self conscious about my own garlic breath and pulled her to her feet. Her additional height just made it easier for me to lean over and suckle her scrumptious breasts. They might be small, but being forced to carry around almost ten pounds on my own chest, I'm of the "more than a mouthful's wasted" school of breast appreciation.

As I clamped my teeth down on Felicia's hard nipple, I saw Eric, stripped of his clothing, return to his knees. His rod stuck straight out.

I guided Felicia over to one of the padded supports, snagging a small pair of cuffs from the wall on my way there. Once I had her secure, I found a larger pair of cuffs and stood by the support opposite Felicia's. I crooked my finger at Eric and he crawled over on his hands and knees offering me a marvelous view of his gorgeous ass. I licked my lips, again.

When I had him cuffed and anchored to the highest tie points I could reach, I retrieved a six-foot signal whip, also a David Morgan, from the wall display. Standing in the middle between my two toys, I could swing the whip and hit whichever of them I was facing. I started gently, just kissing their asses. Felicia moaned and I swear Eric purred. Gradually I increased the strength behind my throws. Felicia's creamy skin turned red pretty quickly. Eric's swarthier hide didn't even show a reaction until I started hitting hard enough to raise welts.

Instead of alternating between them, I changed my pattern so Eric received two strikes for every one I gave Felicia. The tantalizing aroma of her musk mingled with mine, perfuming the room. But then she sagged in her cuffs. Even though Eric looked like he could take a lot more, I needed some relief. Next time, I would start with him, first.

I unclipped Felicia's cuffs and helped her over to the sofa before releasing Eric. With them both kneeling before me, I lifted my legs and each one removed one of my boots and stripped my feet bare. Felicia started with my toes, sucking them into her mouth one by one. Eric licked from the bottom of my feet to my ankles. I couldn't decide who I wanted to lick higher first.

I unbuttoned my shirt and unzipped my jeans. Eric rose on his knees and leaned over, dragging his tongue from the top of my bra to my neck. I moaned. His large hands almost encircled my waist. He lifted me off the sofa just high enough for Felicia to pull down my jeans and soaking underwear, stripping them off. They both inhaled deeply and smiled. I reached behind my back to unhook my bra and Eric pulled my shirt and the bra straps off my arms. With a reverence usually reserved for church, he licked his way down to my nipples, careful to stay to one side so he wouldn't obstruct Felicia who was working her way up my thighs.

I just sighed and reveled in two talented tongues tasting my skin, tracing rings around my areola, and tickling my clit. Felicia had nuzzled her way between my lips while Eric's tongue bathed my breasts. They stayed out of each other's way so neatly, I guessed they'd had some practice lavishing attention on the same woman. I wondered if any of the drawers hid a strapon and a big thick dildo. Of course, then I would have to decide if I wanted to plunge it deep into Felicia's slick cunt or Eric's gorgeous ass.

Enjoying the attention, especially the very human skin-to-skin contact, I allowed them to drive me to not one but three orgasms before I pulled them both by their hair and settled them on either side of me. Stroking Eric's dark mane and Felicia's golden locks, I waited until we all three had stopped panting.

"Would I find a strapon in one of those chests?"

Eric's eyes glittered with excitement again and Felicia dashed over to the nearest one, tugged open a drawer, and extracted a leather harness, several dildos in various sizes, a handful of condoms, and a tube of lube. I took one of the condoms from her, put my hands behind my back, and palmed it in my right hand. Then I put both clutched hands in front of me, fingers down. Felicia dropped to her knees, her arms full of purple, black, and red dildos, and let Eric choose. He picked right and when I turned my hand over to show him the condom, he prostrated himself and covered my feet in kisses.

I selected a double-headed purple dildo and after returning the rest to their drawer, Felicia helped me strap on the harness. I slid one end of the dildo into my dripping cunt, and let her secure it, cover it with a condom, and slather it with lube. I grabbed Eric's hair and guided him so his chest rested on the sofa, one cheek against the leather, watching me out of his right eye. Swaggering over to the wall, I grabbed a lovely, buffalo hide flogger with a couple of dozen wide, 20-inch long strips — Wian by the looks of the handle.

I skipped any additional warmup, walloping Eric's ass until it glowed red, then I slid the dildo so deep inside him my pubic hair tickled his rear. He groaned and I moaned.

I turned to Felicia. "You suck his dick, but he's not allowed to come."

The smirk she gave me let me know Felicia had at least a teensy bit of sadist in her, something I found hilarious under the circumstances. I pulled back until just the tip of the dildo was still inside his ass and walloped him again before slamming all the way back in. Felicia lay on her back, raising her head into his crotch in time with my strokes. I watched his muscles clench, his hands form into fists, his teeth dig into his lower lip. Felicia's slurping, the slap of the leather against his skin, the splurge of the purple dildo reaming his ass combined with our audible panting.

Without releasing Eric's cock, Felicia slid her hand up the inside of my leg and wormed one finger between the harness and my clit. I came hard, my pussy clenching around the silicone rod.

Taking pity on poor Eric who had drops of blood on his lip, I pulled my cock out of his ass, switched condoms, and pushed him aside so I could plunge it into Felicia. Her slender legs encircled my waist, her eyes rolled back in her head, and she lifted her head to wrap her lips around one nipple while her long delicate fingers played with the other. I came again.

"Come for me, girl," I growled. As I suspected she was trained to come on command and immediately convulsed beneath me.

Panting, I fell to one side and lay on the plush carpet, clasping Felicia against my chest. Eric knelt, his ass on his heels, his knees spread, his rod hard and purple.

I nibbled on Felicia's ear and whispered, "I bet you could find me something to hit that with."

She pushed herself to her knees and crawled over to the chest. From a different drawer, she pulled out a five-inch flogger of knobby plastic strands. I grinned and sat up, resting my back against the sofa. I crooked a finger at Eric. He grimaced, but obediently scootched so his swollen cock was within range. The first strike caused his face to scrunch up and by the tenth, beads of sweat appeared on his forehead.

"I beg you, Ma'am. Have mercy. Please either stop or let me come."

I laughed. "Oh, you can come, boy. Just don't make a mess."

"May I, Ma'am?" Felicia looked at his cock and licked her lips.

I nodded and she positioned herself on the carpet in front of Eric. He rose on his knees so his cock hovered just above her open mouth. As I increased the weight and frequency of my blows, the rise and fall of his chest sped up until finally he shouted and his cock twitched, spilling his seed into Felicia's welcoming mouth. She had to swallow twice to consume it all.

I opened my arms and they crawled into them, one on either side. I don't know how long we cuddled there, but my back started to kink. I released them and stretched and Eric lifted me to my feet.

"Ma'am, we have a guest room if you prefer not to travel home this late. We would all be delighted to have you stay and Felicia makes a mean eggs benedict."

"What about Emanuel?"

"He welcomes you in his house, Ma'am." He returned to his knees. "We thought the most comfortable way to handle our relationship would be that when you are in this dungeon, only Eric would come down the stairs. Above, you probably will only interact with Emanuel. Would that work for you?"

I lowered my voice. "What if I want Eric in my bed?"

He shuddered, his cock twitched, and his eyes glazed over for a moment. "I'm sure that could be arranged, at least occasionally."

Felicia knelt on the carpet next to Eric and I stepped between them, putting one hand on each of their shoulders, pulling them against my hips. "I must remember to thank Emanuel for sharing both his delectable toys with me."

Acknowledgements

This book would not have reached your hands without the help of many dear friends and colleagues. I thank my readers and supporters, especially M.K. Blackwind. Thanks also to all those who have served me, well and ill, over the years. I have learned something from each one of you and I hope that you find what you seek.

Other fiction
by I.G. Frederick includes:

Complicated Couplings

Four sexy stories about tangled twosomes

"If You Love Someone" — *Tara leaves her husband to move in with Nathan, but he abandons her after a few months. When he returns, begging her to take him back, life and love look very different.*

"Commiserate" — *The same man dumped them both. When they commiserate, they discover more in common than an ex-boyfriend.*

"Passion's Price" — *Richard steals Gina's heart from three thousand miles away. But, when he moves across the country, her intensity and passion for life drive him away.*

"Lunchtime Lover" — *Both married, they started their affair with the promise never to fall in love. Then Lisa's divorce becomes final.*

www.eroticawriter.net/ComplicatedCouplings.html

Cougar Conquests

Beautiful older women on the prowl and the sweet young cubs captured by their allure

"Benjamin" — A chance meeting at a munch in a tiny town leads Benjamin to an opportunity for training. But, Lady Gina tries to end the relationship rather than emotionally torture herself.

"Festival of Eros" — The handsome young man followed her around all evening, behaving like the perfect submissive ... until she learned his identity.

"Paddles" — A biker bar with no bikers? The decor, name, and patrons of a bar in a small Eastern Oregon town puzzle William who just stopped in for a beer. Then the owner introduces him to the secrets of this very special tavern.

"Starting Over" - When her pet walked out on her, she stayed away from parties because it hurt to watch other women playing with their toys. But, a friend coerces her into attending a unique event.

"The Cougar and the College Boys" — Alone in the woods, hours from Portland, Tess discovers four college friends staying in a nearby cabin. The boys invite her to share their campfire, their dinner, and ...

www.eroticawriter.net/CougarConquests.html

WARNING:

This book changes women's attitudes about relationship dynamics, forever.

In Geneviéve's journey of discovery she dabbles in the BDSM lifestyle which forces her to recognize and acknowledge her true nature. Her memoir, woven together with that of a male slave, draws the reader into an intense odyssey of sexual expression triumphing over sexual repression while delivering fascinating insight about a different kind of love.

"The aptly titled Dommemoir *delivers on so many levels... It quickly sucks you in and envelopes you in the bondage of its spell...* Dommemoir *is a character study that breathes complex and compelling life into its hero, the devastating Lady Geneviéve and the fortunate submissives who worship at her feet... placing you in the delicious bondage of its dark and compelling landscape..."*

Larry Brooks, USA Today bestselling author of
Darkness Bound **and** *Bait and Switch*

www.eroticawriter.net/Dommemoir.html

Eleanor & Mick

A journey of sexual exploration and insight

In five sizzling hot stories, Eleanor seeks refuge in a small town on the Oregon Coast and befriends her younger neighbor. He captures first her heart and then her submission, taking her on a journey of sexual exploration and insight.

"Salt for His Wounds" — When Eleanor's ex-husband shows up begging for a second chance, she asks her young, gorgeous next door neighbor for a favor and Mick takes advantage of the opportunity.

"The Mercantile" — Eleanor attributes Mick's detachment to the difference in their ages, but Mick confesses a need for kink. Afraid of losing him, Eleanor reluctantly consents to bondage and pain.

"The Things We Do for Love" — When her gorgeous girlfriend visits Eleanor on the coast, Mick's obvious attraction troubles her. But, Liz only has eyes for Eleanor.

"Paid in Full" — Mick's army buddy finds Eleanor hot and makes a deal with Mick. But, if Mick really loved Eleanor would he let another man have sex with her?

"Renovations" — After Mick spends a month renovating their garage, Eleanor discovers he built in a few surprises.

www.eroticawriter.net/EleanorMick.html

Family Dynamics

Six sultry stories exploring sexuality in Dominant/submissive liaisons

"'Aunt' Grace" — Jen needed a place to stay in Portland and turned to her father's stepsister. But, she found so much more than she ever dreamed possible with her "Aunt" Grace. Second Place, NLA:I John Preston Short Story Award.

"Leather Family" — Kyle needs his own boy. Jacques would do almost anything to find a place in a Leather Family. But, Kyle serves a female Master.

"Searching" — Two dominants love each other, but need someone who submits to them both. Just how far will young Jeremy go to serve the lovely Lady Theresa?

"Taking Control" — To free the woman she loves from a horrid sadist's perverted games, Melanie must set aside her own aversion to men.

"Family Ties" — When her slave's ex faces eviction, Katherine offers refuge. But can Naomi pay the price?

"Said the Unicorn" — Tessa dedicates herself to her Master's service, so his determination to add another woman to their family devastates her.

www.eroticawriter.net/FamilyDynamics.html

Fork In The Road

Changing people's lives, and relationships
in three pairs of sexy stories

"Said the Unicorn" — Tessa dedicates herself to her Master's service, so his determination to add another woman to their family devastates her.

"Proposals" — The evening appears perfectly arranged for him to pop the question. But, Christopher's proposition takes Geraldine on an unanticipated sexual adventure.

"Winners & Losers" — When he finally walks away from the blackjack table, Jeffrey finds someone worth gambling on.

www.eroticawriter.net/ForkinRoad.html

Ladies in Love

Six sizzling stories of Lesbian Lust

"Empty Seat" — Laura offers Alex a nightcap as thanks for help with a presentation to a prospective client. But they never order drinks.

"'Aunt' Grace" — Jen needed a place to stay in Portland and turned to her father's stepsister. But, she found so much more than she ever dreamed possible with her "Aunt" Grace. Second Place, National Leather Association: International Short Story Award.

"Spa Date" — Dismayed that she introduced Sam to the woman who betrayed her, Julie tries to fix her up again.

"Taking Control" — To free the woman she loves from a horrid sadist's perverted games, Melanie must set aside her own aversion to men.

"Dental School" — How can Cindy flirt with the beautiful blonde dental instructor while her mother propositions the student examining her teeth on Cindy's behalf?

"Commiserate" — The same man dumped them both. When they commiserate, they discover more in common than an ex-boyfriend.

www.eroticawriter.net/LadiesinLove.html

Lessons Learned
Sometimes you need more than love

Four sizzling hot FemDom love stories about women who come to terms with their dominant sides and discover that makes them more attractive to the men they love.

"Tea Party" — What if the first time your best friend drags you to a FemDom "Tea Party" you see your former boyfriend serving canapes naked?

"Blind Date" — How do you respond when you find your ex-husband hanging out at the restaurant where you planned to meet your "Blind Date"?

"To Serve" — If you love a vanilla woman and you only want "To Serve," how do you introduce her to the lifestyle without scaring her away?

"Change in View" — What if a "Change in View" alters the attitude of the man you mentored so he could find his perfect Mistress?

www.eroticawriter.net/LessonsLearned.html

Love Hurts
but in a good way
five steamy stories about the dark side of love

"B&D Trainee" — Online, Xavier promised to make his B&D fantasies come true. But, had he jumped in over his head?

"Knife Play" — Seeking a knife he saw online, Jack inadvertently found himself in a room full of pain and bondage contraptions. He almost turned around and left, but a beautiful woman taught him a different way to appreciate blades.

"Pussy Whipped" — Eric knew nothing about BDSM, but purchased a ticket to a fundraiser to help out his friends. When Miranda asks him to "play," he discovers exactly what those four letters mean.

"The Auction" —He attended the auction with only one goal — to acquire a very special whip. But an offer to try it out proved irresistible and he discovered sometimes events, and women, can exceed one's expectations.

"FemDom Fairy Tale" — A FemDom's offhand remark about a photograph at an erotic art show draws a handsome man's attention. But, when two dominants find each other attractive, which one chooses to kneel?

www.eroticawriter.net/LoveHurts.html

Second Chances

Six sexy stories about getting a second shot at the gold ring

"Back to School" — An admin error forces Jordan and Dennis to share a dorm room. Older than their classmates, they decide to stick together. But Jordan's past threatens to keep them apart.

"Gordon" — When the cover model of her latest book walks into the coffee shop where she writes, Lenore embarrassingly calls him by her character's name. His reaction confounds her.

"Spa Date" — Dismayed that she introduced Sam to the woman who betrayed her, Julie tries to fix her up again.

"Salt for His Wounds" — When Eleanor's ex-husband shows up begging for a second chance, she asks her

young, gorgeous next door neighbor for a favor. Mick takes advantage of the opportunity.

"Proposal — Tangled Webs" — The evening appears perfectly arranged for him to pop the question. But, Christopher's proposition takes Geraldine on an unanticipated sexual adventure.

"Starting Over" — When her pet walked out on her, she stayed away from parties because it hurt to watch other women playing with their toys. But, a friend coerces her into attending a unique event. (Condensed version originally published as "FemDom Party.")

www.eroticawriter.net/SecondChances.html

When Two's Not Enough
Seven sexy ménage stories

"Tribal Fusion" — Whenever and wherever he dances, Dominic collects propositions, but the Lady Lenore's proposal takes him by surprise.

"Two Brothers" — A divorcée in a flashy sports car attracts the attention of two young virgin brothers visiting the "big" city of Boise.

"Honeymoon" — Although she expected to honeymoon aboard a cruise ship, Allison finds herself sailing on a private yacht staffed by an incredibly beautiful couple. Believing her new husband wants to hide

his older, less attractive wife, makes it difficult to enjoy the hedonistic delights offered in paradise.

"Jail Bait" — Serena wants Joshua to pop her cherry, but he won't touch her because of her age. When her birthday finally makes it legal, he arranges for a very special celebration.

"Nikki's Birthday" — Even someone happy in a monogamous relationship might find the gift of a hot, new toy for an evening of decadence incredibly exciting. (Inspired by a real birthday present given to a lovely little bi-sexual, genderqueer slave.)

"Market Boy" — When a beautiful Domme offers Jack the opportunity to serve at a party for her friends, he responds too quickly and too eagerly, getting more than he bargained for.

"The Cougar and the College Boys" — Alone in the woods, hours from Portland, Tess discovers four college friends staying in a nearby cabin. The boys invite her to share their campfire, their dinner, and ...

www.eroticawriter.net/TwoNotEnough.html

Young & Eager
Barely legal but hardly innocent

"Two Brothers" — *A divorcée in a flashy sports car attracts the attention of two young virgin brothers visiting the "big" city of Boise.*

"Teachers Pet" — *Trapped at an all-girls' school in the middle of nowhere, Sabrina tries to get her hunky teacher to bust her cherry.*

"Arresting Development" — *Bethany went out with Officer Rick to avoid a speeding ticket, but discovered she enjoyed getting "arrested."*

"Jail Bait" — *Serena wants Joshua to pop her cherry, but he won't touch her because of her age. When her birthday finally makes it legal, he arranges for a very special celebration.*

www.eroticawriter.net/YoungEager.html

Or visit
http://eroticawriter.net/
to find links to individual stories
and additional collections
and

www.ingramcontent.com/pod-product-compliance
Lightning Source LLC
Chambersburg PA
CBHW061451170626
46811CB00004B/1465